SUPER RABBIT
ALL-STARS!

READ MORE
PRESS START!
BOOKS!

1

3

4

5

9

MORE BOOKS COMING SOON!

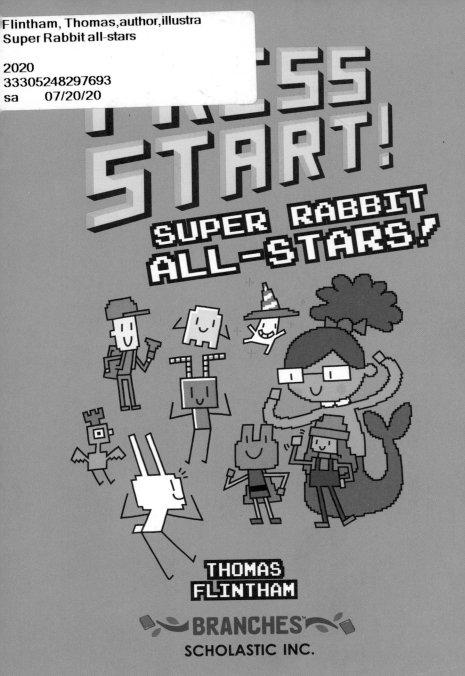

PRESS START!

SUPER RABBIT ALL-STARS!

THOMAS FLINTHAM

BRANCHES

SCHOLASTIC INC.

FOR LEICESTER JOE

Library of Congress Cataloging-in-Publication Data

Flintham, Thomas, author, illustrator. | Flintham, Thomas. Press start! ; 8.
Title: Super Rabbit All-Stars! / by Thomas Flintham.
Description: First edition. | New York, NY : Branches/Scholastic Inc., 2020.
| Series: Press start! ; 8 | Summary: It is time for the All-Star games, and Super Rabbit Boy wants to be crowned the Ultimate All-Star Champion, but with so many contestants, including the evil King Viking, he will need help from Sunny and his video game console to claim his prize.
Identifiers: LCCN 2019007651 | ISBN 9781338239843 (pbk. : alk. paper) | ISBN 9781338239850 (hardcover : alk. paper)
Subjects: LCSH: Superheroes—Juvenile fiction. | Supervillains—Juvenile fiction. | Animals—Juvenile fiction. | Contests—Juvenile fiction. | Video games—Juvenile fiction. | CYAC: Superheroes—Fiction. | Supervillains—Fiction. | Animals—Fiction. | Contests—Fiction. | Video games—Fiction.
Classification: LCC PZ7.1.F585 Sq 2020 | DDC [Fic—dc23 LC record available at https://lccn.loc.gov/2019007651

10 9 8 7 6 5 4 3 2   20 21 22 23 24

Printed in China   62
First edition, January 2020
Edited by Katie Carella and Alli Brydon
Book design by Maria Mercado

TABLE OF CONTENTS

1 PRESS START!................... `1`

2 ALL THE ALL-STARS .... `7`

3 ROUND ONE .... `17`

4 RACE TO THE TOP............ `23`

5 BUBBLE TROUBLE .... `31`

6 BASHING AND BOUNCING ..... `40`

7 DANGER IN THE SEMIFINAL!. `44`

8 A BLAST FROM THE PAST..... `48`

9 THE FINAL ROUND .... `57`

10 NORMAL RABBIT BOY.......... `63`

1 PRESS START!

SUPER
ALL-STAR
GAMES

PRESS START

START
SELECT

It is a Tuesday in Animal Town. The animals are having a party to celebrate.

Suddenly, a star-shaped doorway appears in the sky! A star-shaped creature flies through it.

TO SUPER RABBIT BOY,

   YOU ARE INVITED TO THE SUPER
ALL-STAR GAMES TOURNAMENT! HEROES
AND VILLAINS FROM DIFFERENT WORLDS
WILL FACE MANY CHALLENGES.

   WHO WILL BE CROWNED THE ULTIMATE
ALL-STAR CHAMPION? MAYBE IT WILL
BE YOU!

   WILL YOU JOIN THE FUN? PLEASE
SAY YES.

CHEERS,
KING ALL-STAR

The starby has more invitations to give out.

11

A giant voice booms
down from above.

Welcome to the Super All-Star Games!

It's King All-Star!

Super Rabbit Boy wants to win!

3 ROUND ONE

The Super All-Star Games Tournament is about to begin!

This is how the tournament works:
There will be four rounds of games.
You will all compete in the first round.
Many games will be happening
at the same time.

There will be ten players in
each game. Only two players
from each game will win. Those
winners will move to the second
round of games. Everyone else
will leave the tournament.

Super Rabbit Boy is warped into his first game.

It's a race up Mega Mountain!

The first two players to reach the top will move to the next round!

Everyone speeds up the mountain. Who will get to the top first?

Super Rabbit Boy bounces. He is climbing quickly!

Some of the other racers struggle.

This race is too hard for Slimegirl. She can't jump!

Strong Boy is too slow for this challenge.

That is why I chose a character who can fly!

Super Rabbit Boy is surprised when Wingo flies past him.

See you at the top, bouncing bunny!

Oh bloop!

Just then, a big rock falls down the mountain. It crashes into Wingo!

Wing-NOOOO!

Mega Mole Girl peeks out of a hole.

Whoops! Sorry about that!

Hello, Mega Mole Girl!

Mega Mole Girl is digging a tunnel to the top of the mountain! She is super fast.

Sorry, Super Rabbit Boy. I can't chat now. I'm digging my way to victory!

Super Rabbit Boy is starting to understand that each All-Star has different powers.

I better move fast, or I'll lose this game and be knocked out of the tournament!

Super Rabbit Boy bounces higher and higher. The last part looks hard, but he can see the finish line!

Sky Guy and Angie Crow fly toward the top. They zoom past Super Rabbit Boy.

Super Rabbit Boy has an idea. He bounces
off Angie Crow and Sky Guy toward the
finish line.

Super Rabbit Boy is almost at the top of
Mega Mountain!

Suddenly, Mega Mole Girl pops out of the mountaintop and wins the game!

Super Rabbit Boy makes it to the next round, too.

In a flash of light, Super Rabbit Boy is warped into his second game. He is floating inside a big bubble underwater.

The game starts with a whirl of action! Mega Mole Girl gets thrown out of the water first!

Super Rabbit Boy can't control his bubble because he can't jump.

Pushington Bear swoops toward Super Rabbit Boy.

Just before Pushington Bear can attack, he is grabbed by Crab Queen.

Crab Queen flings Pushington Bear out of the water <u>and</u> out of the game.

Crab Queen spots Super Rabbit Boy. He is her next target!

Before Crab Queen can grab Super Rabbit Boy, Gusty McCloud blows her out of the water!

Next, Gusty McCloud is bashed out of the water by Bashy Boy.

Bashy-bash! Ha! Ha!

Whoooooooosh!

Super Rabbit Boy still can't control his bubble. Worm Kid has the same problem.

This is hard!

I don't know what to do!

Bashy Boy, Super Rabbit Boy, and Worm
Kid are the last three players in the game.

6 BASHING AND BOUNCING

Bashy Boy can't decide who to bash next: Super Rabbit Boy or Worm Kid.

I only need to bash one of you to win. Who will it be?

Super Rabbit Boy and Worm Kid are floating closer to each other. Suddenly, Super Rabbit Boy has an idea!

Bashy Boy sees Super Rabbit Boy and Worm Kid getting closer to each other.

Bashy Boy zooms toward Super Rabbit
Boy and Worm Kid.

Super Rabbit Boy uses his powerful jump
to push away from Worm Kid's bubble.

Bashy Boy is going too fast to stop! He flies out of the water!

Bashy-baaaaaaaaaaaaaash!

Super Rabbit Boy and Worm Kid win the game!

Hooray!

That was a great idea, Super Rabbit Boy!

In a flash of light, Super Rabbit Boy is warped into the hardest game so far. It is full of obstacles, monsters, and traps.

Everyone jumps into action!
There are dangers everywhere.

King Jump
gets caught in
a spider's web!

Mister
Super Cool
falls through a
trapdoor!

King Viking is captured by a ghost gorilla!

It flings him out of the tournament.

Super Rabbit Boy bounces past fireballs, jumping snakes, and spike pits.

The Dude Bros use their dude moves.

Billip appears in front of the Dude Bros.

Billip taps both Dude Bros with his glowing gloves.

Suddenly, the Ooze Monster attacks! The Dude Bros try to use their moves . . . but they can't.

Billip has stolen the Dude Bros' special dude moves! He flips and slides to safety. The Dude Bros are out of the game!

No way!

Not fair!

Wow! I did not know Billip can take powers from other characters and use them as his own!

That is what Billip does!

Super Rabbit Boy is getting tired. Luckily, he is far away from Billip.

Billip keeps stealing powers.

Without their powers, the other All-Stars lose quickly.

The semifinal is over. Billip and Super Rabbit Boy made it through to the final!

Wow, that was fast! What happened to everyone?

Billip blip!

I'm surprised I made it!

Ha! No one is laughing at us now!

In a flash of light, Super Rabbit Boy is warped into the final round of the Super All-Star Games!

Boing! Boing! Where am I now?

The final game is . . .

GRAB THE ALL-STAR CUP!

There can only be one Ultimate All-Star Champion!

Super Rabbit Boy and Billip race to find the All-Star Cup! Billip has lost the powers he stole in the last round.

Super Rabbit Boy leaps to a high platform.

He sees Billip down below.

He spots the cup. It is really high up!

Before Super Rabbit Boy can bounce, Billip appears. He taps Super Rabbit Boy with his glowing glove.

Super Rabbit Boy tries to jump, but he just falls down. He has lost his jumping power!

Billip may have taken Super Rabbit Boy's power, but Billip doesn't know where the All-Star Cup is.

Super Rabbit Boy can't jump anymore, so he climbs instead.

Billip bounces around looking for the cup. He does not see it anywhere.

But Super Rabbit Boy keeps climbing. He is getting closer to the All-Star Cup!

Billip looks up and spots Super Rabbit Boy nearing the All-Star Cup. He uses his new jumping power.

Super Rabbit Boy climbs as fast as he can. But he is just a normal Rabbit Boy.

Billip has almost caught up to him.

Super Rabbit Boy has an idea. He lets go and falls into the air!

Super Rabbit Boy lands on top of Billip!
Together, Super Rabbit Boy and Billip zoom
toward the All-Star Cup.

They both
reach out and . . .

Super Rabbit Boy grabs the All-Star Cup first! He has won!

THOMAS FLINTHAM

has always loved to draw and tell stories, and now that is his job! He grew up in Lincoln, England, and studied illustration in Camberwell, London. He lives by the sea with his wife, Bethany, in Cornwall.

Thomas is the creator of THOMAS FLINTHAM'S BOOK OF MAZES AND PUZZLES and many other books for kids. PRESS START! is his first early chapter book series.

These All-Stars are somewhere in the story. Can you find them all?

Spingy

Eye Guy

Astro Pete

Little Knight

Flame Kid

PRESS START!

How much do you know about
SUPER RABBIT
ALL-STARS!?

All-stars from many different worlds are asked to join the Super All-Star Games Tournament. Who is invited from Animal Town?

 Super Rabbit Boy is worried about the BUBBLE BOP game. Why does he think this game will be hard for him?

Who wins Mega Mountain Climb? How does this character win? Reread Chapter 4.

 Who is the only character not cheering for Super Rabbit Boy at the end?

Super Rabbit Boy, Mega Mole Girl, Worm Kid, and Billip do well in the tournament. If you were Sunny, which character would you choose? Which game would you play? Write and draw your own action story.